MONTY + SYLVESTER

A TALE OF EVERYDAY SUPER HEROES

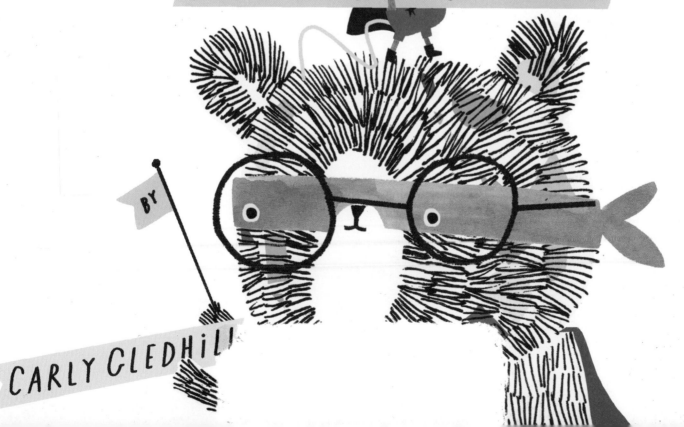

BY

CARLY GLEDHILL

FOR NICK - C.G.

ORCHARD BOOKS

First published in Great Britain in 2018 by
The Watts Publishing Group
This edition first published in 2018

1 3 5 7 9 10 8 6 4 2

Text and illustrations © Carly Gledhill, 2018

The moral rights of the author have been asserted.

All rights reserved.

A CIP catalogue record for this book is available
from the British Library.

HB ISBN 978 1 40835 174 1
PB ISBN 978 1 40835 175 8

FSC MIX
Paper from
responsible sources
FSC® C104740

Printed and bound in China

Orchard Books
An imprint of Hachette Children's Group
Part of The Watts Publishing Group Limited
Carmelite House, 50 Victoria Embankment
London EC4Y 0DZ

An Hachette UK Company
www.hachette.co.uk

www.hachettechildrens.co.uk

MONTY + SYLVESTER

A TALE OF EVERYDAY SUPER HEROES

CARLY GLEDHILL

YEAH!

ORCHARD

MEET MONTY AND SYLVESTER.
THEY'RE SUPER HEROES (IN TRAINING).

MONTY IS READING
THE SUPER HERO MANUAL.

SYLVESTER IS WORKING OUT.

FOUR IMPORTANT STEPS TO BECOMING A SUPER HERO

(TAKEN FROM THE MANUAL)

STEP 1
STAR JUMPING

INVISIBLE PANTS READY!

STEP 2
RESEARCHING

HOW TO BE A SUPER HERO

GOT THE OUTFIT, READ THE MANUAL.

STEP 3
LUNGING

MASK TO HIDE IDENTITY

STEP 4
SELF DEFENCE

KARATE KICK!

AFTER ALL THAT PRACTICE IT'S TIME TO GO
OUT AND **SAVE THE WORLD...**

... IF ANYONE
NEEDS THEM TO.

TUMBLEWEED →

THE PHONE IS RINGING. THIS MEANS SOMEBODY NEEDS HELP!

IT'S TIME.

AWAY THEY BRAVELY GO.

IT'S A CLASSIC. STUBBORN CAT, STUCK UP A TREE.

BUT THERE IS NOTHING WRITTEN IN THE MANUAL ABOUT THIS,
WHAT ARE THEY GOING TO DO?

OH NO!

HANG ON A MINUTE, I'VE GOT A GREAT IDEA!

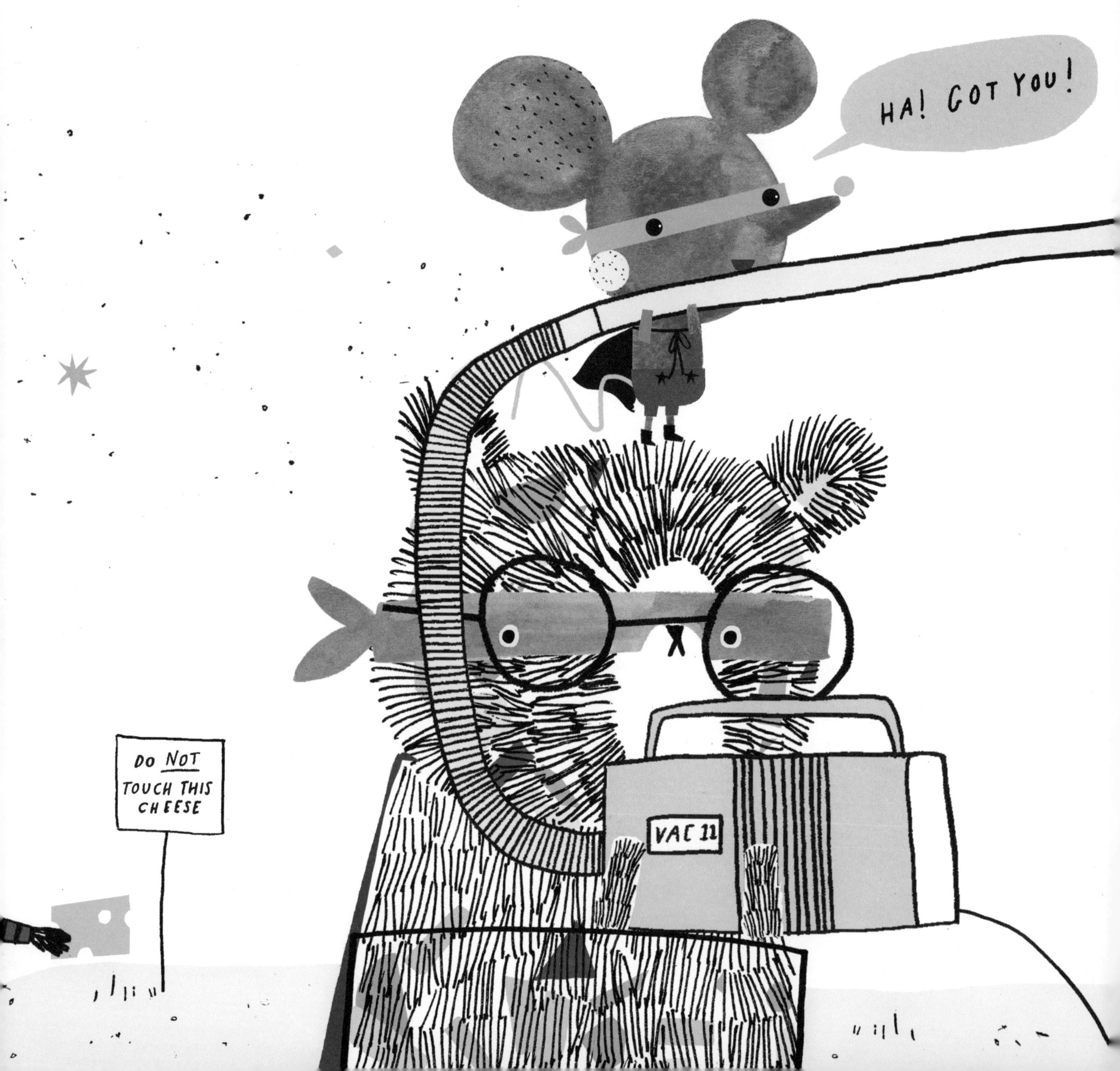
HA! GOT YOU!
DO NOT TOUCH THIS CHEESE
VAC 11

USING THEIR TRUSTY VACUUM CLEANER
THE PROBLEM IS QUICKLY SOLVED.
FIRST MISSION COMPLETE!

WOAH!

PHEW! WHAT A GOOD IDEA, WHO KNEW THAT A VACUUM CLEANER COULD BE SO HELPFUL TO A SUPER HERO.

THEY THINK
THEY'RE CLEVER,
DON'T THEY!

THE PHONE IS RINGING AGAIN,
IT'S TIME FOR THE
NEXT MISSION!

THE VACUUM CLEANER IS REALLY HELPING.

NO VILLAIN IS A MATCH FOR MONTY AND SYLVESTER.

LADIES AND GENTLEMEN, PLEASE FASTEN YOUR SEATBELTS.

SOON THERE IS NO PROBLEM TOO LARGE FOR THE PLUCKY SUPER HEROES.

VAC 11

I MUST PUT A STOP TO THESE DO-GOODERS IMMEDIATELY.

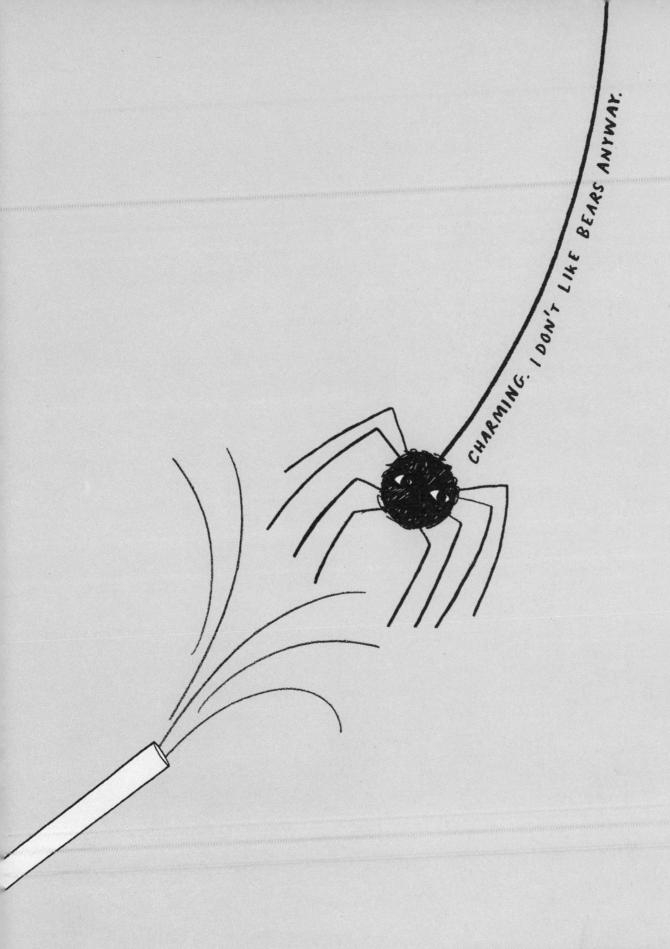

IT IS ALL GOING SO WELL UNTIL...

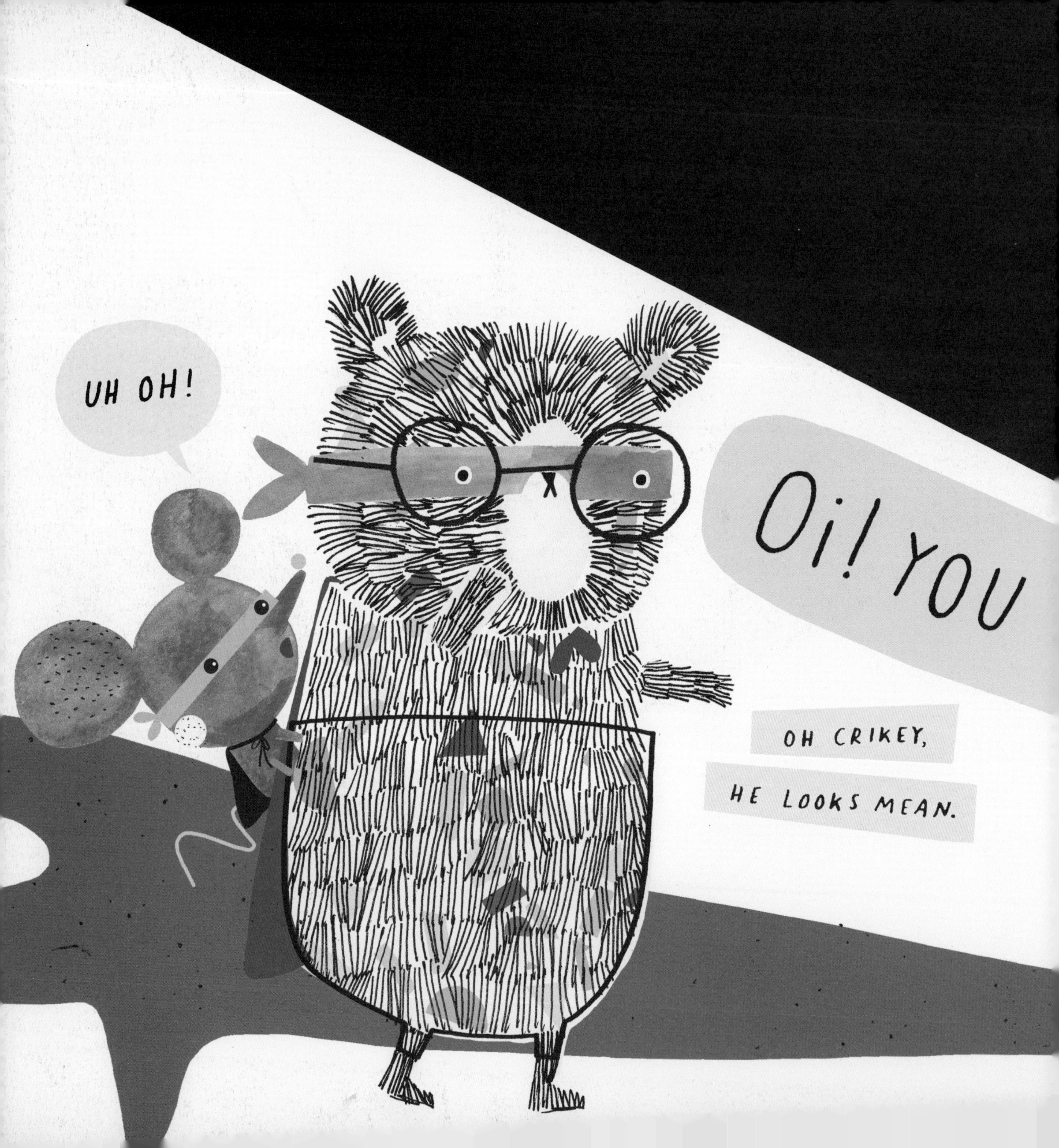
UH OH!
Oi! YOU
OH CRIKEY,
HE LOOKS MEAN.

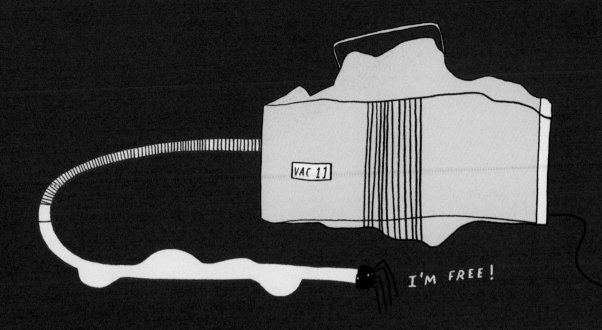

I'M FREE!

YOU THINK YOU'RE SO CLEVER BUT YOU'RE NOT! YOU CAN'T RELY ON A VACUUM CLEANER TO DO YOUR DIRTY WORK. I'M IN CHARGE NOW AND YOU HAVE TO STOP!

TWO. BUFFOONS!

EVIL SPOTLIGHT

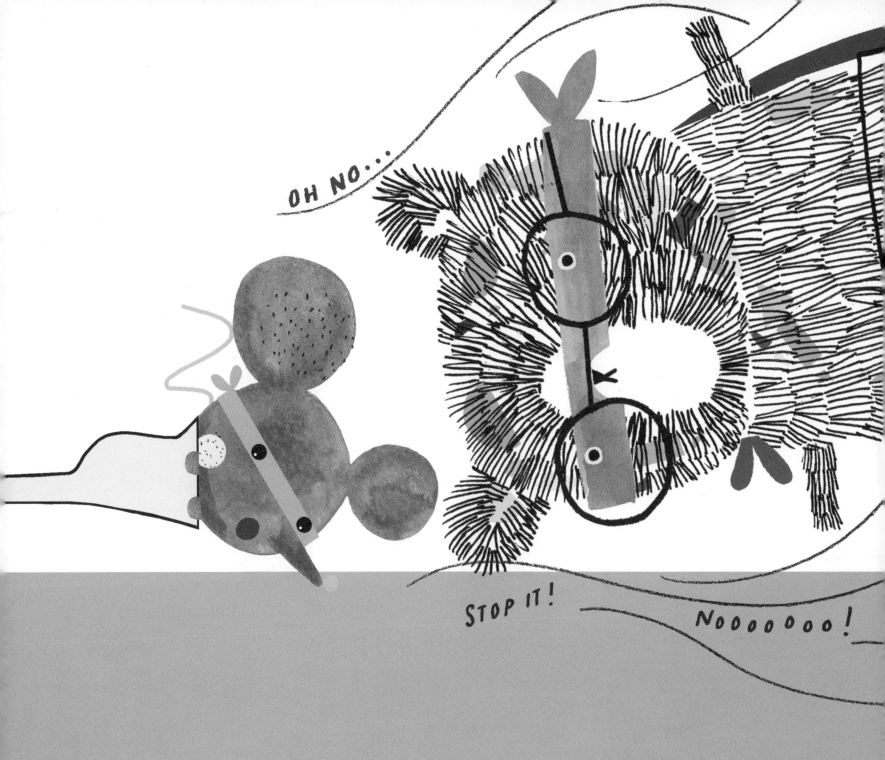

OH DEAR, THIS DOESN'T LOOK GOOD.
HOW ARE THEY POSSIBLY GOING TO ESCAPE?

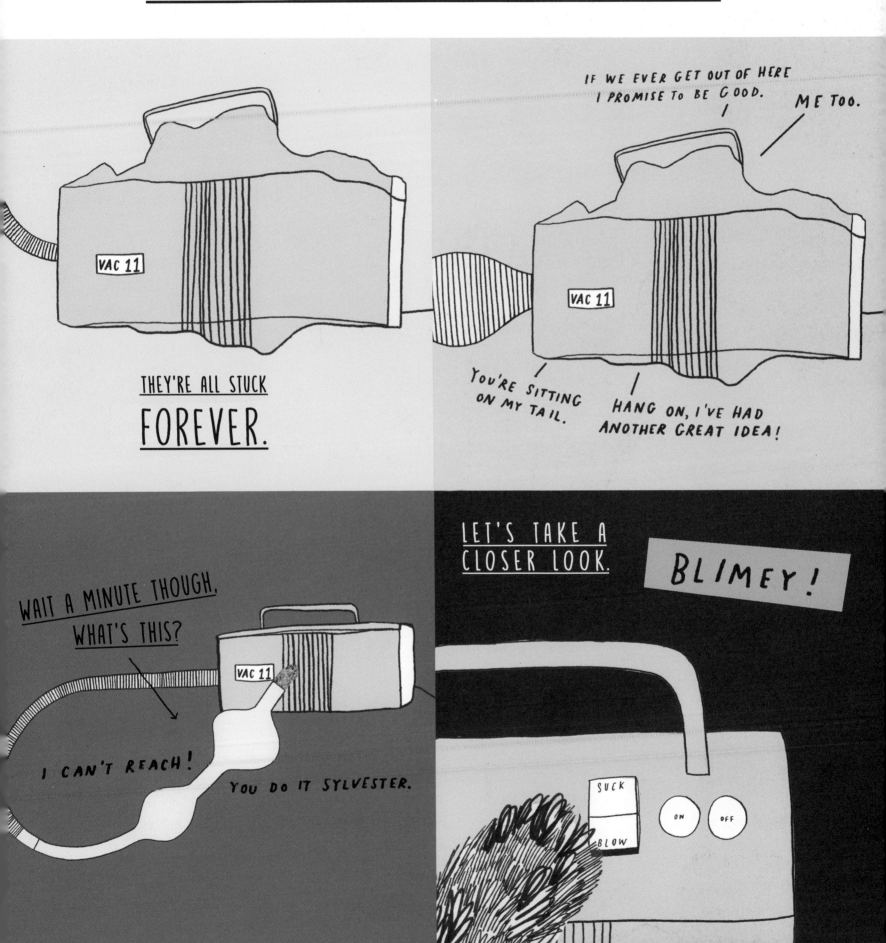

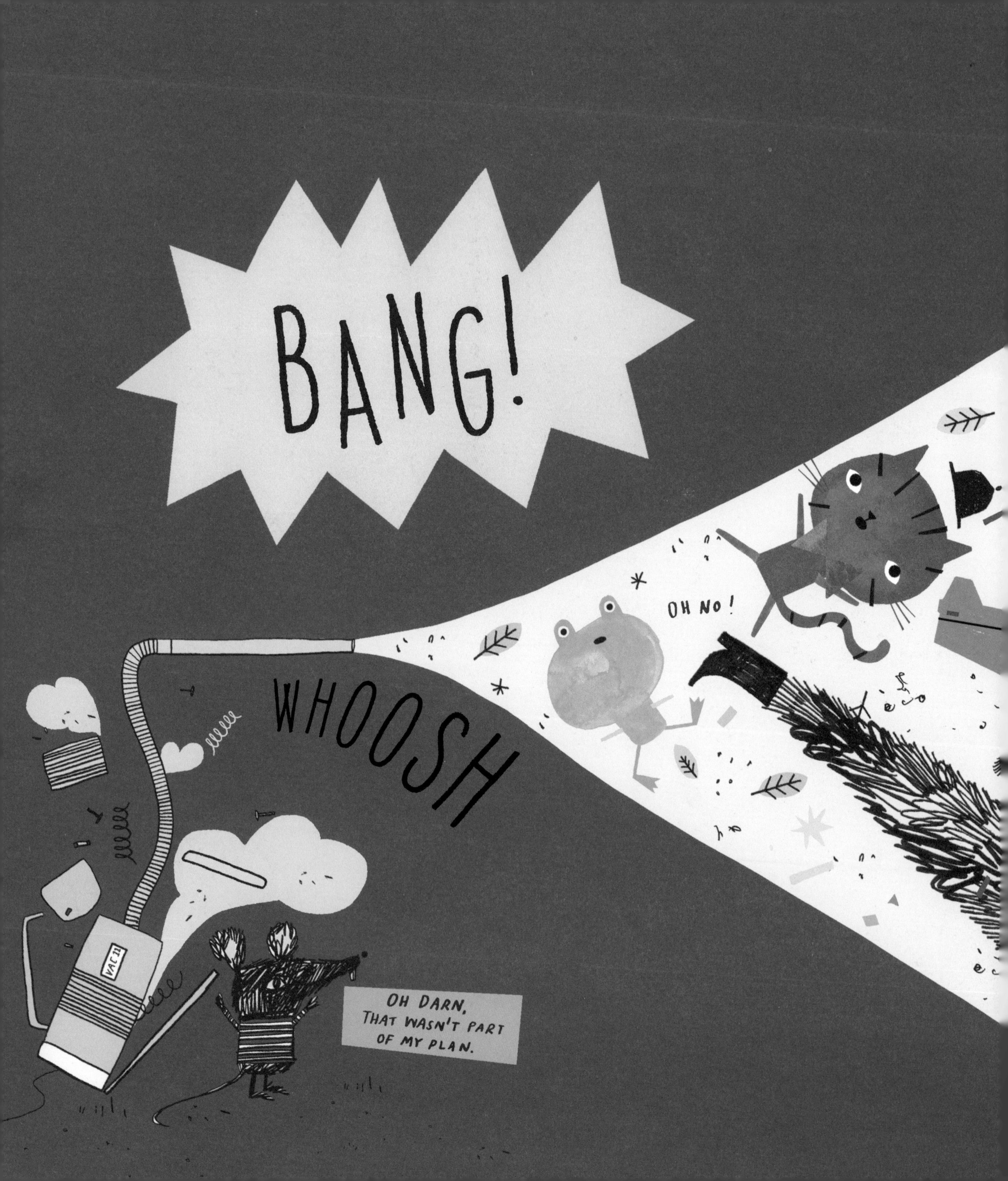
BANG!
WHOOSH
OH NO!
VAC 11
OH DARN,
THAT WASN'T PART
OF MY PLAN.

HOORAY!

POW POW POW!

...BECAUSE THE NEXT TIME THE RED PHONE SOUNDED THEY WOULD HAVE A FEW EXTRA HELPERS!

THE END

A TOPNOTCH JOB WELL DONE.
MISSION COMPLETE!
TIME TO PUT THEIR
FEET UP, WATCH TV,
EAT SOME CAKE...

TO DO:
BECOME SUPER HEROES ✓
CAPTURE BAD GUY ✓
SAVE WORLD ✓

...WAIT A SECOND.

YOU NEED US

WHERE?